A Wolf For Christmas

AMY LAURENS

OTHER WORKS

Find other works by the author at
www.amylaurens.com

A Wolf For Christmas

INKLET #48

AMY LAURENS

Inkprint PRESS

www.inkprintpress.com

Print ISBN: 978-1-925825-47-3
eBook ISBN: 9781393738862

www.inkprintpress.com

National Library of Australia Cataloguing-in-Publication Data
Laurens, Amy 1985 –
A Wolf For Christmas
64 p.
ISBN: 978-1-925825-47-3
Inkprint Press, Canberra, Australia
1. Fiction—Fantasy—Romantic 2. Fiction—Romance—Paranormal—Shifters 3. Fiction—Fantasy—Paranormal
4. Fiction—Holidays 4. Fiction—Short Stories

First Print Edition: December 2020
Cover photo © Jakob Owens via Unsplash
Cover design © Inkprint Press
Interior art © Amy Laurens

A WOLF FOR CHRISTMAS

"**K**ITTY," DOUG SAID AS HE STOPPED AT the far side of the all-white kitchen, beige towel slung low around his hips, dark hair still damp and tousled from the shower. "Why does my lounge room smell like dog?"

I shrugged nonchalantly from my spot on the thick grey rug, trying to keep the sparkle from my eyes and the nerves from my heartbeat—and trying not to give in to the temptation to hunker down out of sight behind the wrap-around couch. *Please don't hate me,* I thought at him. *Please don't hate me.*

It was possible, of course, that he already did. He'd been gone six months after all, and everyone knew the front lines changed people, messed with their heads, broke them down.

Oh, he'd seemed okay for the most part since he'd returned, a gleam still there in his amber eyes, the hint of a strut in his walk, confidence in the set of his strong, well-defined shoulders.

But he hadn't wanted to be close to me for long, hadn't wanted to touch me, and the voices that had been slowly growing in volume for the last half a year reached fever pitch: *He doesn't love you anymore. He found someone else. Someone who knows what it's* like.

Doug inhaled deeply, doing all sorts of pleasant things to his chiselled pecs and shoulders, and snorted. "I can definitely smell dog."

The white benchtops in the kitchen were so clean they practically sparkled in the light from the skylight; the floor was almost a mirror with its polished white tiles. I could still vaguely catch the scent of the pine-o-fresh floor cleaner I'd used two hours ago, though it was mostly overpowered by the smell of the roasting leg of lamb in the oven (marrying Doug had definitely made my regular senses sharper, that was for sure, even if I was as locked out as ever from anything supernatural).

The lamb even had a homemade basting sauce, and there were root vegetables currently browning nicely, and I had things out on the stove to make gravy in another few minutes.

I was kind of proud, to be honest. I'd learned a lot since Doug had been away.

Hopefully he'd be proud, too.

The small, four-person dining table in the far corner near Doug was cleared for a change, and covered in a white-ish table cloth; the couches were clean, and I'd even moved them to vacuum underneath.

I shrugged from where I sat on the rug in between the three sides of the couches, my back to the switched-off TV. "I don't see anything in here that could smell like dog."

Quickly, I shifted my leg, deliberately knocking against the white laminex TV cabinet to cover the little snuffling noise behind me.

Doug sharpened, senses alert. "What was that?"

I shrugged, but I couldn't keep the edges of my grin contained—or my nerves. "No idea." This *was* a good idea, wasn't it?

Dammit. The poor little thing was going to freak out, like they all did, and then what was I planning to do? I was an idiot. A blithering, insecure idiot who—

Doug sniffed disbelievingly and stalked closer, abs and towel both shifting as he did.

An idiot who was easily distracted. That was me.

Mmm. Six months was a long damn time.

"Kitty," he said in a soft growl, dark amber eyes pinning me to the spot. "What have you done?"

Two years we'd been married, and we'd dated for another three before that—and I still couldn't move when he did that stare, frozen in place by instinct older than civilisation, the reaction of all squishy prey when the wolf prowled toward them. Except the chills down my spine weren't bad—they weren't bad at all, and I could feel heat pooling in various strategic locations of my body.

The quick flicker of the corner of Doug's mouth said he could smell just exactly how much I wanted him.

Come on, I thought, straining as though I might be able to reach his own thoughts with mine. *Take me up on it this time. Please.*

Three days he'd been home, with barely a hi-how-are-you hug.

I shoved the voices back down into the murky depths of my soul and shifted my shoulders back to give him a better view of my chest.

He rounded the corner of the lounge, pushed me gently back down as I half rose to meet him, and let the towel fall to the mat.

I inhaled deeply, sifting past the smells of clean city-pipe water and lavender soap to the man beneath, earthy and rich and wild.

Yes. Yes yes yes. Thank you. At last. Yes please. Yes.

Behind me, a large red-and-white box under the belated Christmas tree squeaked.

Instant mood killer.

Doug went stiff again—as in, his *whole* body, thanks very much—and narrowed his eyes over my shoulder. "Kitty," he said slowly as he let one hand drop feather-light down my shoulder.

"Mm?" Hard to concentrate on his face when his hand was doing that.

Six months. Did I mention that?

"Why is one of the presents whimpering?"

I sighed deeply, shoulders slumping, and turned to face the presents with him—with at least the small consolation of being able to press my back against his clean, naked, exceptionally well-muscled front. Ha. "Probably," I said, "because it's confused."

"Not as confused as I am," he muttered. Abruptly, he retrieved his towel, twined it around his waist again, crossed to the glittering plastic tree that cost more than a week's worth of my wages, and plonked onto the floor.

I sighed again, muttered to myself—
down girl, down—and went to join him.
I leaned against the grainy black-and-
white weave of the couch that still
smelled faintly of accidental chilli, one
of my legs sticking off the mat onto the
tiles that chilled the back of my bare
calf. Pleasant. The air con was doing a
rip-roaring job of keeping the indoors
bearable, but it was still mid-summer
hot.

"Kitty," Doug said, shifting so his
bum was between my knees, then lea-
ning back on me, head tucked between
my breasts, "why is the box that's
addressed to me shaking?"

It was, of course. The poor thing
had only been in there for ten minutes,
and it had been nicely sleepy, but I
guess being stuck in a dark box would
be enough to put anyone on alert.

Stupid idea. It could probably sense
Doug's presence and was already getting freaked out.

"Just open it," I said, suddenly flat.

"I'm not sure I want to."

"I know," I said, letting my head fall back against the lounge and closing my eyes.

Christmas had been and gone more than a week ago, anyway. Most people around here were already done celebrating New Year's. It had been stupid and whimsical of me to try to make this a proper celebration, and suddenly the grief of having been alone without even weekly phone calls for six months was too heavy to ignore any more.

"You better let it out," I said, voice heavy and tired. "It probably needs to pee."

Doug stretched out a long arm, snagged the box, and brought it onto his lap. "I can't believe you bought me a dog," he muttered, without even a hint of amusement. "You know it's just going to go berzerk as soon as it smells me."

I shrugged, still mostly pinned in place by his warm weight.

There was the scuff of the box's lid being pulled off, and Doug froze.

I cracked one eye open. My heart melted all over again at the tiny bluish-grey, velvet-furred something-something-bulldog popping up in the box.

Doug snorted. "Kitty, that's the ugliest dog I've ever seen."

I elbowed him aside and scooped the tiny furball up out of its soft blanket in the box. "Don't be ridiculous," I said. "She's adorable." I snuggled her to my face, her blue-grey fur velvety against my cheek. "She'd be dead if I hadn't taken her in," I added.

Doug practically whirled around on the spot. "You adopted a stray?" He shimmied backward as I though the thing I held was contagious. "You know I'm allergic to—"

"Does she look like a stray?" I demanded, holding her up by my face.

I mean, sure, she smelled doggy, but it was *clean* doggy. And she'd come with vaccination records and everything.

She licked my eyebrow, and I giggled.

Doug's body language relaxed a little. "No. She looks like a bloody purebred French bulldog, and I'm terrified to even ask how much you paid for her."

I hefted her around in front of me so I could take a good look. "French bulldog? I thought she was just some weird kind of mix."

"Lady," Doug said, "I know my canines."

I snorted and snuggled the puppy back into my lap, drawing my knees up. "She was at the pound," I said as she licked my fingers. "Someone had dumped her not even a week after Christmas. I paid their adoption fee, that was it. She's vaccinated and certified flea-free."

"Good," Doug said vehemently, trying to hide the shiver that went down his spine every time someone mentioned fleas. Doug and flea-rid products weren't a good mix, see, because of his weird allergy, and every time—

The kitchen timer interrupted, agreeing with the deep, savoury smells from the oven that the food was just about done.

"Here," I said, passing the puppy over. "Watch her while I finish lunch."

Doug took her reluctantly, grumbling—but his touch was gentle, and despite his frown, he snuggled her down into his towel-covered lap just as neatly as I had.

I snorted. "Well, she's certainly not running screaming from you, is she?" I said as I entered the kitchen.

I pulled the oven open to do a visual check, and steam engulfed me momentarily in a hot but delicious wonderland. I don't care what anyone says, rosemary on roasted potatoes is its own kind of magic.

Couple more minutes. Just long enough to make the gravy. I closed the oven door, straightened, and glanced over at Doug.

He stood on the rug, frowning down at the puppy in his arms.

His towel was slipping again.

Wow had I missed those hip bones.

I just wanted to—

"Why *isn't* she running and screaming?" Doug interrupted. He glanced up at me, amber eyes troubled.

I shrugged. "I don't know, maybe she likes wolves. Probably thinks she is one," I added as the tiny pup gnawed at my husband's thumb.

Carefully, slowly, Doug bent over and put the puppy down—back into the box, from judging by the little scratching sounds her nails were making, though I couldn't see over the back of the couch.

I tore open the new packet of gravy powder and dumped it unceremoniously into a small pot on the stove. The instructions on the back of the box suggested a cup of water, so I turned, reaching for the drawer with the measuring cups—and ran smack into Doug's chest.

He caught me, lacing the fingers of his left hand through my right, clutching me tight against him, body taught, eyes troubled.

"What?" I said, gaze flicking from left eye to right eye to left again. "What's wrong?" Anxiety flared in my chest. "I'm not getting rid of her," I said, voice firmer than I felt. Something in Doug's eyes was setting me adrift, and I scrabbled, seeking something solid to stand on. "She was at the pound, Doug. If someone doesn't keep her, they'll kill her, and she's not exactly the cutest puppy on the planet, and I—"

"Hush," he said, drawing me even closer and bowing his head over my shoulder. "Shh. It's okay. You can keep the puppy."

I struggled against his grip, fighting to move back so I could search his face again. "Then what? What is it?"

He swallowed, hard, Adam's apple stretching and relaxing. "I—"

The acrid smell of burning gravy powder wound around us. Dammit. I didn't remember turning the stove on—must have done it out of habit.

I twisted to turn it off.

Before I could, the string holding Doug up snapped.

He collapsed against me, face crumbling, sobbing for air, and when I couldn't hold him, he slumped to the floor, me with a death-grip around his biceps, trying to slow him down a little.

There was a thump from over by the Christmas tree.

"I'm sorry," Doug gasped as his shoulders shook.

I wiped my hand firmly over his cheek. It came away wet. "What?" I said, adrenalin raging through my chest. "What's wrong? Why are you sorry?"

What have you done?

I had just a second to hate myself for that last thought before something grey and approximately the size of a giant plug-in vacuum cleaner barrelled into us.

I blinked.

Colour me stupid, but I was approximately 99.99999% sure I'd bought us a puppy for Christmas, not a garbage-bin sized, blindingly steel-coloured *thing* with ears a bat could be proud of.

But Doug was clinging to it, his arms wrapped around its neck, sobbing into its shoulder, so... hey. What the heck.

Cautiously, I joined in the hug, wrapping one arm around Doug's shoulders before letting my other hand skim the dog's silvery side.

As I did, energy crackled along my fingertips, something like static electricity, but stronger—and suddenly, I *felt* stronger.

Not physically. Physically I was the same as always, or at least, the same as New!Me, who'd been going to the gym four times a week while Doug had been away in an effort to keep myself busy and give him a value-added version to come home to.

Damn insecurities.

So no, not physically stronger, but internally.

All the uncertainty and loneliness of the last six months was washing away, like silt lifting from the bottom of a pond, and I could sense my *self* underneath, solid as bedrock, unshakeable.

Of course Doug still loved me.

He *loved* me.

The sparkly magical doom puppy slopped its tongue all over my face, washing away with it the last of the silt on my soul.

It seemed to be having a similar effect on Doug; he'd stopped shaking, and was wiping his face—though admittedly he was mostly using the dog—puppy—*thing* to do it.

He sat up, inhaled shakily, and smiled at me—a watery, hesitant thing that set off new worries in my chest right as I'd been thinking about getting up to shut the stove off.

Gravy powder wasn't flammable, was it?

I crouched, reaching up for the knob of the stove—and blinked at the small cloud of smoke hazing over the stove-top. Oops.

I switched the stove off quickly—and Doug tugged on my other hand, pulling me back down with him as he shuffled so he could lean against the dishwasher. He tucked me in under his arm, and the dog-puppy-thing curled itself up under his other arm, and he took me by the chin. "It's been a hard few months for you, hasn't it?"

I shrugged. "Not as hard as it's been for you."

Doug smiled wryly. "Yeah." He drew in a deep breath and expelled it, stronger, calmer. "But it won't happen again."

"What do you mean?" I asked, confusion wrinkling my face. Doug was one of the top agents his pack had. He was clever, he was stealthy, he was strong… They'd never lost a battle yet when Doug was involved. So why would they suddenly let him retire? "What's going on?"

Doug's jaw twitched. "I…" Another deep breath. "Kitty. Kit. Katherine."

I stilled, liquid fear swirling through my gut. He never called me Katherine.

He tipped his head back against the smooth metal of the dishwasher's door, his throat smooth and strong and exposed. "They can't use me anymore," he said. "I'm done."

"Done?" My frown deepened as the burning smell thickened, the smoke slowly drifting outward from the stove. "But how can you be *done*? How—"

"We met someone there," he said. "Someone we didn't expect to meet. She..." He swallowed, and from this angle, with his throat tipped back like that, it struck me for the first time that, wolf or no wolf, ultimately he was just a man—just as vulnerable as the rest of us if you caught him off his guard.

"The puppy's not scared of me," he said softly without opening his eyes, or moving his head.

I snorted, glancing down at the beast that was still as big as half a

Labrador, though it seemed to be shrinking slowly as I watched. "Gee," I said. "Magic wonder dog isn't afraid of a big bad wolf. I'm so shocked."

He tilted his head toward me, eyes still closed. "Did you know it was a magical wonder dog?"

"Me?" My eyebrows skyrocketed. "Of course not. She was just the last one left at the pound. I felt sorry for her. I wanted something warm and alive to… to keep me company next time you left. She made me feel loved," I murmured, heart tearing in five directions at once: the rawness of admitting the truth, the grief that Doug would feel like I felt he didn't love me enough, the realisation that the damn dog had probably made me feel like that on purpose so I would bring it home…

I growled. "They did warn me she was a bit special. I thought they were talking about how ugly she is."

Doug smirked. "I told you she was ugly."

"Shut up."

He gave his head a shake and squeezed me close. "Anyway. That's..." He sighed. "That's not why she's not afraid of me."

I tried to frown up at him, but he was holding me too tight.

"I told you. We met someone there, someone we hadn't expected, and she... She had abilities we didn't count on."

"But everyone's okay, right?" I said slowly. He'd seemed relaxed when he'd gotten home, satisfied, and he'd been joking and laughing...

I thought about the spark of cold I'd felt from him, the tiny jolt of electric fear that maybe I'd been right, maybe he'd found someone better, someone more like him, and didn't need me anymore. "Right?" I repeated, suddenly desperate for confirmation.

"Kitty," he said softly. "I'm not a wolf anymore."

The room was whirling, spinning so fast my vision blurred. "What... what do you mean?"

"I'm not a wolf anymore. That's why the dog's not afraid of me."

Smoke stung the inside of my nostrils. I snorted it away.

"She was a sorceress," Doug whispered into my hair. Even so, I could hear the fear in his voice. "She..." His hand crept up, fingers twining through my hair, lips pressing hard against my scalp. "She cured my curse."

"It's not a curse," I said reflexively—and it wasn't, it never had been, it had been a choice, something Doug had gone into willingly with his eyes wide open at the age of fifteen when he'd seen what magic was doing to the world and had stepped up to try to help stop it. Not everyone was able to be made into a shifter—not all of us were born with the ability to interact with magic—I was as blind as a naked mole rat about anything magical, I couldn't help, I couldn't do anything except marry someone who could, and support him as best as *I* could—but Doug had been practically born for it.

Doug the Dog, his mates had called him.

He'd been born for it.

"Can they fix it?" I asked—because I had to, not because I had any hope. He wouldn't have broken down like he had if there'd been a way to fix it.

He shrugged, a tiny shift in his grip as he clung to me like a life raft. "I… I wondered if… there might be. But… The dog's not scared of me, Kitty. There's nothing left to heal." His voice cracked. "You know the procedure can't be repeated."

And it was true. Animals, unlike humans, didn't need help to sense the magical energies that were tearing the world apart, and—unlike humans—they couldn't seem to sense the difference between the people who were trying to ruin the world, and the ones who were trying to stop it.

I'd never known a dog not to be cautious of Doug.

I'd bought one anyway, to feed my own need for affirmation—not deliberately, but on a whim, because I'd seen the silver-blue pup lying there in her straw and she'd looked so adorable, so helpless, and I couldn't do anything to fight the larger battles, but by God I could fight the small ones and keep her safe.

I glanced at her again, now nearly back to her original size and flopped like a silvery-grey puddle of fur on the tiles at Doug's side. "I think I was had," I muttered.

"What?"

"The dog," I said. "I never planned to get one. I wouldn't really do that to you, not if I was thinking straight. I think I was had."

Doug laughed, just a little, just softly, and scooped the sleeping puppy into his lap. "I guess she needs a name if she's staying," he said.

I rubbed my hair off my face and grinned at him. "I think we all know what her name is."

He frowned at me, but it was a small, superficial thing, lightweight, mundane, and it lightened the weight in my chest to see it. "What?" he asked.

I grinned harder. "Wolf," I said. "Someone needs to fulfil that role in the family, don't you think?"

Doug stared at me for a minute, then pressed his face against my shoulder. "I love you," he murmured.

"I know," I said. "I love you too."

"I thought you might leave me," he breathed against my neck, words as light as air, as heavy as night.

"I thought you already had," I whispered back as I ran my fingertips along the outer edge of his ear.

"Never," he said firmly.

"I know."

THE MAKING OF
A WOLF FOR CHRISTMAS

This story started with the cover image, actually. I was browsing for images for the 2019 Inklets and found the photo of the silver-grey puppy in the Christmas box. There was another image, a similar one but with a little curly-haired wheaten pup, and I had this grand idea that Liana Brooks and I might write matching Christmas stories and release them with matching covers…

Yeah. You can laugh. It's totally okay. Go ahead.

The joke here, of course, is that getting Liana to write a short story at all is like getting a cat to treat you like an equal: it happens randomly, sporadically, unpredictably and on whatever topic the lightning inspiration struck with.

And honestly, I'm not much better.

So that plan was cursed from the outset—but I had the images, and they were too good to waste.

All I had was a woman in a kitchen/lounge area that looks suspiciously like my Mum's house in my head, and a puppy in a Christmas box. Everything else grew organically out of that as I sat down in our main character's head and typed what she was thinking.

To be honest, the idea of the magical war is really intriguing, and I love the (unplanned) idea of the government recruiting people to become shifters to fight in the war. One day, I might explore this world further.

For now, I hope you enjoyed this.

DOWNLOAD YOUR FREE EBOOK

When you buy a print book from Inkprint Press, we like to say THANK YOU by offering you the ebook for free!

Please head to
www.inkprintpress.com/inklets/48/
and the use the coupon INK48LET to get your copy of this Inklet in epub AND mobi today!
(Coupon will only work once.)

Read more by Amy Laurens!

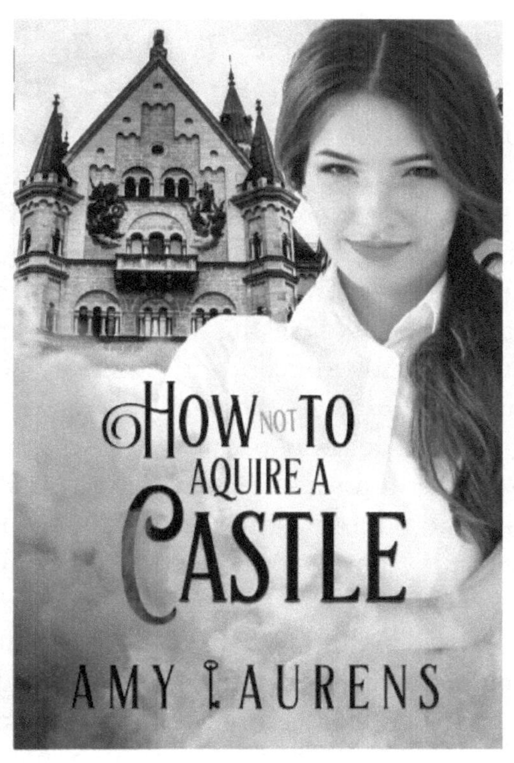

HOW NOT TO ACQUIRE A CASTLE

CHAPTER ONE

ON A HARD PLASTIC CHAIR IN THE FRONT row of the Great Hall in the world's fifth-best evil overlording academy, with its red-wooden parquetry floor that spoke of wealth and the beige, square panels of sound-boards speaking of conservatism on the walls, Mercury sat, pointedly not sweating.

Partly, this was because the Academy Administrators had deigned to turn on the air-conditioning earlier in the day, in recognition of the fact that the hall would be packed out with approximately six hundred bodies, all here to celebrate the graduation of about a third of that crowd.

But mostly, Mercury was pointedly not sweating because she made it a point never to sweat, sweat being an indication that she was working hard, and hard work being antithetical to her way of life.

However. If she *had* been sweating right now, it would not have been due to the uncomfortable warmth of six hundred packed bodies that even the air-conditioning system couldn't completely shift, or, in fact, from overexertion. Instead, it would have been caused by an even more unfamiliar concept in Mercury's emotional vocabulary: nervousness.

Mercury did not *get* nervous. Mercury got things *done*.

So the fact that she was sitting here, in the front row of the Great Hall, about to graduate from Evil Overlording Academy (with distinction), and was feeling *nervous*... She crumpled the black paper program in her pale fists. It made her furious, that's what it did.

Abjectly furious, that snooty-tooty Deviran with his stupid morals and his stupid I-don't-want-to-be-here and his stupid Overlords-are-empty-figureheads and his stupid face sitting ten people over, looking implacable with his deep brown skin and barely-there, precision-groomed beard, as though he knew it gave him a stupid air of alluringly stupid mystery…

Mercury scowled and searched for the train of thought that had been derailed, yet again, by Deviran's stupidity.

Ah. Yes. She was angry because she was nervous because she wasn't absolutely entirely one hundred and fifty percent sure that she'd beaten Deviran in their final exams, and 1) being anything less than a hundred and fifty percent certain of anything made her cranky, and 2) being beaten by Deviran for dux of the year would be utterly unbearable. She flicked away a piece of fluff that had become snagged under her immaculately magenta-painted nails and smoothed out the black paper program.

In the front corner of the hall, the starkly-attired string quartet with their traditional black instruments began playing the March of the Oncoming Doom. The screechy scrapes of hundreds of chairs on the hall's wooden floor sounded as the crowd climbed to its collective feet.

Mercury sat with her arms firmly folded for a few moments longer, until her best friend Sparky kicked her in the ankle.

"Get up, idiot," Sparky hissed, hints of real flame flickering through her flame-coloured pixie cut.

"No," Mercury said, flouncing to her feet and tossing her own glossy brown hair back over her shoulders. Four years she'd been playing by the Academy's rules in order to get what she wanted, and she'd had just about enough. Other people's rules should only be applied to plebs too stupid to invent their own.

Sparky rolled her eyes somewhere over Mercury's head before focusing on the stage, where the ceremonial party had begun entering.

Mercury clenched her jaw and narrowed her own eyes as the teachers of the Evil Overlording Academy filed onto the stage, dressed in their formal finery. Each teacher had their own distinctive look that matched their personality and their Overlording style, from severe charcoal suits to jet-black leathers, pastel ball-gowns and gem-toned lingerie and eye-blinding spandex, and even on one tiny old woman at the back, worn jeans and a grey flannel shirt. She was the one to watch out for, of course; Mercury could respect an Overlord who was confident enough in their abilities that they didn't need to telegraph them. It wasn't a look *she* would consider, of course, but still. She could respect it.

The band's march finished and, after a moderately awkward pause, the crowd sat. The Principal, pale skin and dark hair matching his suspiciously vampiric red-and-black suit, took the podium, and Mercury narrowed her eyes. He was doing a superb job of hiding his emotions—he was a premier Evil Overlord, after all—but she was Mercury, and unlike anyone else, she had the benefit of being able to rummage through people's consciousnesses. She was better at adding things *into* people's minds than taking information out, but he was telegraphing fear loudly enough that she could sense it without trying overly much.

Mercury pursed her lips.
Hmm.

The Principal cleared his throat at the blackened-wood podium, and the fear made it into his usually-unreadable eyes. "Before we begin," he said, and Mercury's stomach did a peculiar kind of flip-flop. "I have a pressing announcement to make regarding the safety of our students and their families."

He cleared his throat again and took out a sheet of paper from his pocket, unfolding it carefully and smoothing out the creases before beginning again. "The Council"—quiet booing echoed around the hall, and Mercury tsked impatiently— "have asked me to recommend that students from Tumul Tuos seriously consider postponing their return to town for a few days. The city is dealing with a *situation* at present which may present a danger to our students' health and safety."

Mercury's hands fisted at her sides and she forced herself to remain seated. What was wrong with her city? What had the Council mucked up now? A risk to the students' safety? There had to be more he wasn't telling them. Gently, Mercury tugged on his consciousness, implanting the suggestion that it might be better to share the news than to keep it secret. After all, how could they fight an enemy they didn't know?

"There are, ah…" He trailed off, glancing side to side as though wondering why his mouth had decided to continue.

Mercury didn't snicker, but she did press her lips together in satisfaction.

The Principal took a deep, steadying breath and seemed to change tack. "There has been one death already. The family have already been notified, so it is with much regret that I must inform you that Woovermyer will no longer be with us at the Evil Overlording Academy."

Murmurs broke out around the room, not all of them sad—to be expected in a school devoted to raising the next generation of dictators (ish) and despots (of sorts).

Mercury, however, crushed her program in her left hand, fist so tight her nails bit her palm.

"You okay?" Sparky murmured.

Mercury gave a single, tense shake of her head and stared at the podium. Dead. Livie Woovermyer was dead in *her city*. And the Council hadn't done anything to stop it. Couldn't do anything to stop it, probably, given they'd warned the students to stay away. Livie hadn't been the strongest candidate in the year level, but she was no lightweight, either. It would take a lot of power to kill a Seven.

Enough was enough. A good thing Mercury was about to graduate at the top of the class, giving her the right to knock the lowest ranking current Overlord off their perch. Tumul Tuos would be hers in a matter of hours. And then there'd be no more of these wasteful deaths. Her city would be safe at last.

Madame Pompadour was up the front now, elbow gloves the same glimmery silver colour as her elaborate, piled-curls wig, eyelids gleaming with matching silver eye shadow, and abruptly Mercury realised Madame was there to make the announcement that would change her life forever. She leaned forward in her seat, ready to stand when her name was called.

"And now the announcement you've all been dying for," the Political Alliances teacher trilled, the frills on her evening gown fluttering as she moved. "The dux of this year's cohort!"

Sweat slicked Mercury's palms. Irritated, she reached over and wiped them on Sparky's thigh.

Sparky pushed Mercury's hands back into her own personal space bubble and Mercury, nervous to the edge of distraction, let her.

"Will you please join me in welcoming to the stage, our wonderful dux for this year, Deviran Goodsmith!"

Mercury froze halfway to standing. "Did she just say Deviran?" she whispered furiously to Sparky.

Sparky hauled her forcibly back down into her seat. "Yes," she hissed back. "Sit down, you're making a fool of yourself."

Mercury's spine snapped upright as she sat, and she arranged the folds of her long black skirt demurely. "No I'm not." She closed her eyes. "Deviran's going up to the stage, isn't he?" Even at a whisper, the misery in her voice was clear, but this time, she didn't care.

Sparky reached over and squeezed her hand.

Mercury squeezed back, lacing her fingers through Sparky's, and held tight as all her plans and dreams vanished in front of her.

A stone had landed in her chest. That must be it. Some strange sort of magic that made her chest contract and sink, and made the world distort for just a moment, long enough to trick her into thinking Deviran had beaten her so that someone could jump in front of her and yell SURPRISE!

Any moment now.

Any moment.

She refused to open her eyes and watch Deviran parading across the stupid stage like some stupid stupid-person, receiving his stupid medal and stupid symbolic crest pin.

It was that last exam question.

She'd known Deviran would pull out his ridiculous 'Evil Overlords are merely figureheads, the Business Guild is where the power really lies' rant that everyone had heard a million times back when he was younger and angrier, and she'd tried to counter it, she really had.

She'd argued for the importance of the Overlording position, for the power of having a symbolic figure to unite the population in their hatred, for having a person able to make all the difficult, necessary decisions the Council was too weak and spineless to make... But it hadn't been enough. Everything she'd worked for, everything she'd set out to prove—and it wasn't enough.

There were words, there were names, and then forever later, once she'd died twice already, Sparky elbowed her in the ribs. "Come on," Sparky muttered. "We're up next."

And sure enough, there was a shuffling of presenters as the last of the Powers Behind The Thone graduates departed the stage, and the next speaker announced in

threatening, funereal tones, "The Overlording cohort."

Mercury blinked furiously and followed
Sparky to the end of the line at the right
side of the stage. The other candidates
proceeded one at a time across the stage,
two girls and then stupid Deviran, and
then a handful more and then Sparky, and
then the speaker was calling her name.

Hands fisted, Mercury tossed her head
high, climbed the four steps, and marched
across the stage. She wouldn't look at
them, the stupid faculty who'd denied her
the city she rightfully deserved, and she
wouldn't look the other way either, at the
classmates and crowd undoubtedly snig-
gering at her failure.

She shook hands with the presenter,
and while he pinned the tiny crossed-
swords badge on her collar, her eyes
betrayed her and slid towards the aud-
ience. Her stomach flipped as she saw the
crowd of parents and friends behind the
rows of students, all the way to the back
of the hall, twenty rows at least, illum-
inated by the late afternoon light stream-

ing in through the ceiling-high windows to the right. Everyone had someone here to watch them graduate. Everyone except Weird Al—and her.

The presenter finished with her pin, muttered something to her, and offered his hand again. Mercury coldly ignored it and strode from the stage. It didn't matter. None of it mattered. Tumul Tuos was her city anyway, and no one could change that. She'd think of something. She'd take a day or two out, make some plans…

And she could always hope that Deviran would choose some other Overlording territory. He'd be stupid to, but then again, he was stupid, so. Mercury could hope.

All at once, mid-way down the steps off the stage, Mercury came to rigid attention, scanning the room. Somewhere out there in the crowd, an exchange of power had just taken place, and it felt… unusual.

But the final few students were backing up behind her and muttering, so Mercury headed back toward her seat, craning her head all the while and searching for some sign of whatever it was that had just discharged a dizzyingly quiet amount of power into the room.

She sat, and Sparky leaned over. "Okay?"

"Mm," said Mercury. "Did you feel…" She accidentally caught the eye of the student behind her and twisted back to face the front.

"Feel what?"

Mercury turned it over in her mind. It had felt like a large shot of power discharged very quietly—but perhaps it hadn't been. Perhaps it had only been a small discharge after all, something most people wouldn't have noticed.

But still, something about it had tugged on her. It very nearly felt like something she'd felt before, only she *knew* she'd never sensed that kind of discharge before.

She shook her head. "Never mind. Don't worry."

Sparky sighed and straightened. "It's fine, Mercury," she said, drily exasperated.

"I know you didn't win, but I promise, you'll live through it."

Mercury waved a hand for silence.

The power had just discharged again, and it had come from somewhere in the back corner, far away from the windows and light.

Impatiently, Mercury waited for the formalities to conclude. The crowd stood while the quartet played the exit march, and the stage party left, Mercury tapping her foot all the while.

The moment the last notes of the march died away, Mercury turned and headed to the back corner, weaving in and out of the students and parents who had seemed to explode slowly but inexorably out from the neat rows of seating, ignoring Sparky's calls behind her. Power, something that tugged in a way that was strange and familiar, all at once. She pushed her way through a family posing for pictures—and halted.

In the shadows of the back corner, Deviran stood with his family, with his stupid, smug little smile, looking as tall and dark and stupidly alluring as ever. Prat.

His mother, short but sleek, and his father—tall, and utterly terrifying in a way not at all diminished by his gleaming smile—gushed over him, patting his back and hugging him tight. Within moments the Principal was there, glibly shaking hands and congratulating them on the success of their son. Something flickered across his consciousness, and also Deviran's father's—some moment of recognition in response to what they were saying.

But Mercury brushed it aside just as the mother brushed melodramatic tears from her cheeks and handed Deviran a silver-wrapped package about as long as her hand but half the width.

That. That was the source of the strange, magical feeling. Mercury watched hawk-eyed as Deviran un-wrapped the gift. A glimpse of gold set her pulse racing—What was it? What did it do? Could she steal it?—and then the paper fell away to the floor, and Deviran stood staring wordlessly at the object in his hands, and Mercury did too.

Wide-eyed, Deviran raised his gaze to his parents, and even from where she stood Mercury could hear the reverence in his voice as he thanked them.

But Mercury had eyes only for the object. No wonder she'd felt it discharge, and no wonder it had felt both strange and familiar. In Deviran's hands lay a glorious, sunshine-gold key, large and strong—and with a handle in the shape of a stylised fish, long, flowing fins curving to make the grip.

A Key. They'd given him a Key. And not just any Key, but *the* Key, *her* Key, the Artefact of Power belonging to *her* city.

A wordless noise of wanting rose in Mercury's throat. Who cared about being dux? She needed that Key.

Keep reading! Head to
www.amylaurens.com/books/
kaditeos/castle
to buy your copy now!

ABOUT THE AUTHOR

AMY LAURENS is an Australian author of fantasy fiction for all ages. While she has never owned an *actually* size-indeterminate dog, her giant Labrador *was* entirely confused about how large he was.

Amy has also written the award-winning portal-fantasy *Sanctuary* series about Edge, a 13-year-old girl forced to move to a small country town because of witness protection (the first book is *Where Shadows Rise*), the humorous fantasy *Kaditeos* series, following newly graduated Evil Overlord Mercury as she attempts to acquire a castle, the young adult series *Storm Foxes*, about love and magic and family in small town Australia, and a whole host of non-fiction.

INKLET #031
Welcome to Dark Dale
LIANA BROOKS

INKLET #032
When War Came to Town
A Powers Story
AMY LAURENS

INKLET #033
Not Fantasy
AMY LAURENS

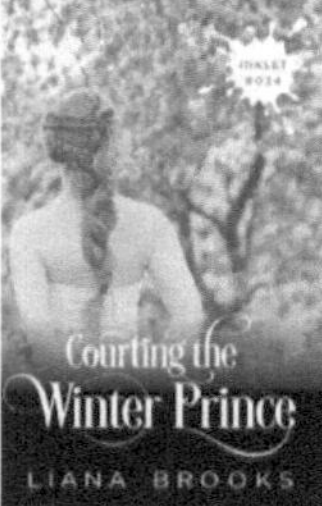

INKLET #034
Courting the Winter Prince
LIANA BROOKS

INKLET #035
At the Home of the Winter King
A Storm Foxes Story
AMY LAURENS

INKLET #036
With This Ring
AMY LAURENS

DOUBLE ISSUE
INKLET #037
Venus & Seven Reasons I Said No
LIANA BROOKS

INKLET #038
OATH KEEPER
AMY LAURENS

INKLET #039
FORGET
A Powers Story
AMY LAURENS

INKLET #040
NOT QUITE Cinderella
LIANA BROOKS

INKLET #041
ONE BAD MAN
AMY LAURENS

DOUBLE ISSUE
INKLET #042
The Claustrophobia Of Loneliness &
Adam, Be A Star
AMY LAURENS

INKLET #043
The Artist as a Young Girl
LIANA BROOKS

INKLET #044
CONFESSIONS
AMY LAURENS

INKLET #045
But For Snow
A Kaditeos Story
AMY LAURENS

INKLET #046
The Boy Named NO
LIANA BROOKS

INKLET #047
Anamata
AMY LAURENS

INKLET #048
A Wolf FOR Christmas
AMY LAURENS

www.ingramcontent.com/pod-product-compliance
Lightning Source LLC
Chambersburg PA
CBHW031035190726

48286CB00003BA/1195